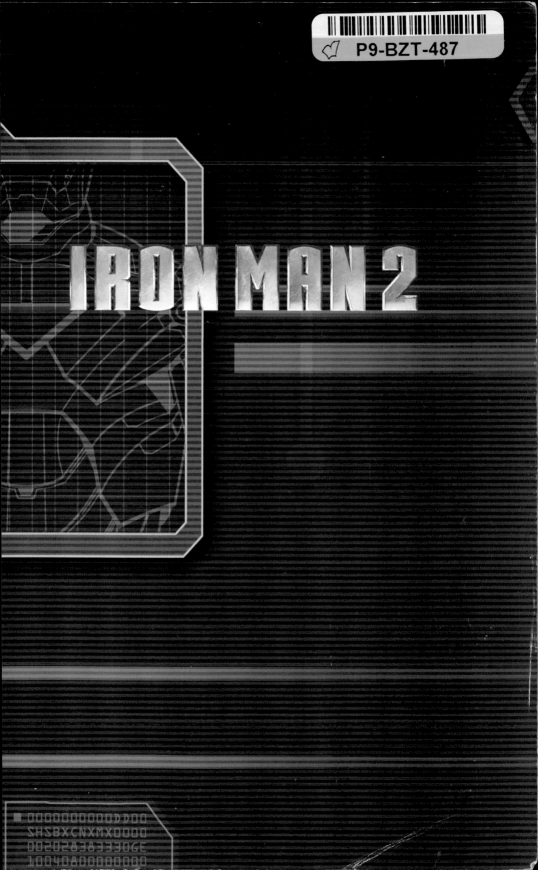

IRON MAN 2

■ 0000000000000000
SHSBXCNXMX0000
00202838333306E
10040800000000

Little, Brown and Company

Hachette Book Group
237 Park Avenue, New York, NY 10017

Visit our website at www.lb-kids.com

Little, Brown and Company is a division of Hachette Book Group, Inc.
The Little, Brown name and logo are trademarks of Hachette Book Group, Inc.

First edition: April 2010

ISBN 978-0-316-08366-9

10 9 8 7 6 5 4 3 2 1

CWO

Printed in the U.S.A.

IRON MAN 2

IRON MAN'S FRIENDS AND FOES

Adapted by LISA SHEA

Based on the screenplay by JUSTIN THEROUX

Pictures by DARIO BRIZUELA

Inked by MIGUEL SPADAFINO *and* LEANDRO CORRAL

L B

LITTLE, BROWN AND COMPANY

New York   Boston

When you are rich and famous,
you make lots of friends.
But you make lots of enemies, too.
The trick is to know the difference!

Tony Stark is rich and famous.
He is also known as Iron Man.
He invented the Iron Man suit
to help keep the world at peace.

Tony runs Stark Industries.

He used to make weapons, but not anymore.

Justin Hammer runs a rival company,

named Hammer Industries.

Hammer, instead of Tony,
now sells weapons to the government.
But Hammer is jealous of Tony
because Tony has the Iron Man suit.

WHO CAN MAKE AN IRON MAN SUIT?

Lieutenant Colonel James T. Rhodes
is Tony's best friend.
Tony calls him "Rhodey."
They used to work together.

Rhodey works for the government.
When Tony stopped making weapons,
Rhodey started working with Hammer.
Tony doesn't like that.

Pepper Potts is Tony's assistant.
She helps him with everything,
even when he's Iron Man.
She is always there when he needs her.

Pepper is so good at her job
that Tony gives her a promotion.
Pepper is thrilled!

Pepper isn't the only friend who's always there for her boss. Happy works for Tony, too.

12

Happy is a bodyguard and limo driver, and he does anything else Tony asks. He even helps Tony practice boxing!

Natalie Rushman is a paralegal.

She works for Tony's company.

Natalie is pretty.

She is smart, too.

Tony offers her Pepper's old job.
Pepper does not like that idea,
but Natalie happily accepts.

Tony invites his friends to go to a car race.
When they get there, Tony discovers
that some of his foes are also there.

Justin Hammer shows up.

Hammer owns a car, too.

But Tony has a big surprise.

He is one of the race car drivers!

A strange man walks onto the track
during the race.
His name is Ivan Vanko.
Cars crash around him.

Ivan shouts out loud,

"You come from a family of thieves!"

He wants to hurt Tony.

Ivan has a repulsor on his chest. It is like the one Iron Man wears. Ivan uses it to power whips on his arms. He calls himself Whiplash.

The police capture Whiplash,

but he soon escapes from prison.

He runs off to set his evil plan into motion.

Agent Coulson and Nick Fury
talk to Tony about Whiplash.
They work for S.H.I.E.L.D.
The group fights bad guys,
such as Whiplash.

A woman in dark clothes joins Tony and Nick. Tony cannot believe his eyes — she is Natalie! Her real name is Natasha Romanoff. She works for S.H.I.E.L.D., too.

Rhodey sneaks an old Iron Man suit onto an Air Force base.

Weapons are added to the suit, turning it into a War Machine.

Rhodey says the suit is top secret.

It should be used only in an emergency.

But a general issues an order:

he wants the new suit shown to the public.

Pepper and Happy attend an expo.
People show off their new inventions.
They see Rhodey in the
War Machine suit.

There are some new robots on display.
No one knows where they came from —
no one except Whiplash.
He built them to start trouble.

Surprise! Iron Man drops in.

Iron Man was tracking Whiplash.

He knows that the villain built the robots.

He knows that the robots are dangerous.

He's right — the robots start to fire!
Even the War Machine suit
takes aim at Iron Man!
Rhodey can't control it!
He warns his friend
to watch out.

There are too many robots
for Tony to handle alone.
Even in his Iron Man suit,
Tony needs help from his friends.

Pepper and Happy are there to help. The S.H.I.E.L.D. agents show up just in time to join the battle, too. Iron Man knows that with friends like these, he will always win.